For Jean Weinfeld

Dikou and the Baby Star
Copyright © 1988 by Elzbieta
All rights reserved.
No part of this book may be used
or reproduced in any manner whatsoever
without written permission except
in the case of brief quotations embodied
in critical articles and reviews.
Printed in Belgium.
For information address Thomas Y. Crowell Junior Books,
10 East 53rd Street, New York, N.Y. 10022.
Published simultaneously in Canada by
Fitzhenry & Whiteside Limited, Toronto.
10 9 8 7 6 5 4 3 2 1
First American Edition

Library of Congress Cataloging-in-Publication Data
Elzbieta.
   Dikou and the baby star.

   Translation of: Dikou et le bébé étoile.
   Summary: Little Dikou tries to take care of a
baby star until his parents tell him to return it
to the hills where he found it.
   [1. Stars—Fiction]   I. Title.
PZ7.E563De 1988   [E]   88-302
ISBN 0-690-04719-3
ISBN 0-690-04721-5 (lib. bdg.)

Translated from the French by Leslie A. Kimmelman and Lynda Cassanos
Translation © 1988 by Harper & Row, Publishers, Inc.

DIKOU
AND THE
BABY STAR

Elzbieta

Thomas Y. Crowell New York

One summer night, little Dikou left home and set off toward the hills. The farther he went, the darker grew the night and the dimmer the stars.

Finally he couldn't see anything at all. "If I had known," Dikou said, "I would have stayed in my soft little bed. It's so dark out here—there isn't even one star to light my way."

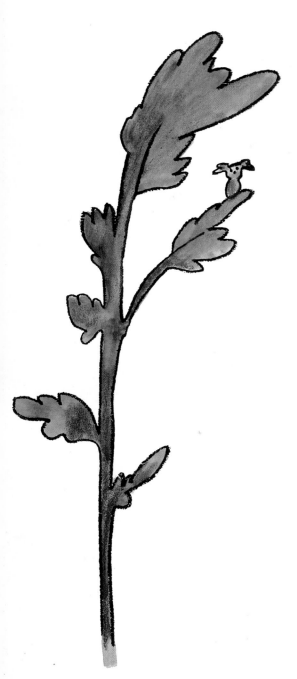

He was starting to feel scared when suddenly he saw something sparkling in the distance. When he got closer, he found a small shimmering light perched on the leaf of a tree.

"Could this be a baby star that has fallen from the sky?" he wondered. "Maybe its parents are looking for it right now."

Dikou waited a bit. The little star twinkled from time to time, but no one came.

"If I leave it here all alone, it will die," thought Dikou. "I'll take the star home with me and bring it up as my baby. Then, when it is all grown up, I'll have my own star in the sky."

And that very night, Dikou found his way home, thanks to the light of the little star.

The next day, Dikou asked his father, "Papa, what do stars eat?"

"Gold and silver, I suppose," Papa replied absentmindedly.

"A lot?"

"Go ask your mother," Papa said. "Can't you see I'm busy!"

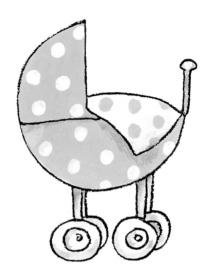

So Dikou asked his mother, "Mama, what do stars eat?"

"Lettuce leaves, I guess, but you should go ask your father."

"Papa said they eat gold and silver," said little Dikou. And Mama replied that it was possible—since stars shine so brightly.

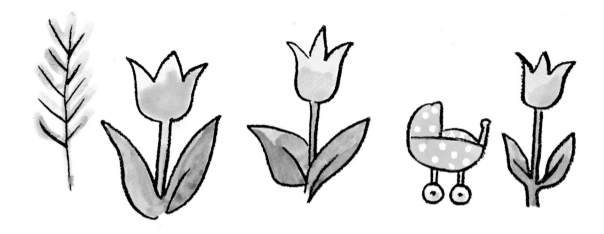

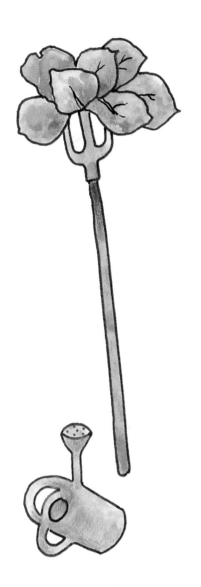

Dikou gave a lettuce leaf to the baby star. But he asked himself, "Where will I find gold? Where will I find silver to make my star shine?"

That night it seemed to Dikou that his baby star was dimmer than the night before. So he took Mama's silver spoon from the kitchen drawer and told his star to eat the silver if it wanted to grow up big and shiny.

The next morning, Mama came to Dikou. "Who told you that you could take my silver spoon?" she scolded. And she took back the spoon.

That night Dikou said to himself, "My star doesn't like to eat salad. It needs gold or silver. It is already dark outside and my baby star is hardly shining at all."

So he took Papa's gold watch and gave it to the star, saying, "Eat this, my little star, if you want to grow up to be big and shiny." And he added, "Don't be afraid of Papa. He'll never even notice that you have nibbled at his watch."

But the next day Papa cried, "Who told you that you could take my gold watch? This child is impossible! First he takes a silver spoon, then a gold watch. What next!" And he took back his watch.

Night came, and the little star didn't shine at all.
Dikou was heartbroken. "My baby star won't light!
My baby star is dead!" he sobbed.

"What is going on here? Can't we have any peace and quiet in this house?" said Papa.

"It's all right, Papa," Mama said. "It's just Dikou's shiny piece of glass. He thinks it's a real star. Besides, if you hadn't told him that stars eat gold and silver, he wouldn't have taken our things."

"Oh, fine, I see that this is all *my* fault," grumbled Papa. But he smiled and added, "Let's go see what we can do for this baby star."

That evening, Mama, Papa, and little Dikou walked through the woods and up the hill where Dikou had found the star.

When they reached the top, Papa said, "And now, Dikou, we are going to send your little star back into the sky where it can grow big and shiny."

He lit a firecracker that was attached to the faded baby star. The firecracker soared into the night.

Then something amazing happened. In the place where the firecracker had disappeared, an enormous star burst into the sky. It whirled and swirled, beaming rays of silver and gold. Little by little, the star became smaller, until all that was left of its blaze was a tiny twinkling light.

Mama, Papa, and Dikou waited for the little light to fade away. But it just kept shining, all night long. A new star had been born.

"Well," said Mama, "so it wasn't just a piece of shiny glass."

And little Dikou was happy. He knew that, because of his family, there would never again be a night without stars.